SCIONS

—— OF AN ——

ENIGMA

Gabriel Anthony Lopez

Inquiries and Book Orders should be addressed to:

Great Writers Media
Email: info@greatwritersmedia.com
Phone: 877-556-0487

ISBN: 979-8-89175-047-0 (sc)
ISBN: 979-8-89175-048-7 (ebk)

CONTENTS

I

"You know what it's like to find a star outside," said Byeolsu.

He and Tati were sitting outside the old Imperial Council chamber in Orgoz. Byeolsu took Tati's hand and put it in his and held their thumb up to the star covering it. Byeolsu was convinced that he loved Tati. They both had met under similar circumstances over year ago in the twilight of Charybdis II. Charybdis II gave up much and put on a show of lights from both its mother nature and the firmament. Fireflies can be seen in the distant meadows. For Byeolsu and Tati, they would sleep soundly; but unknown to them, Charybdis II was now capable of giving something else up—their lives.

In the brisk morning, Byeolsu was ready to play some games of bainet with Tati. They put on the necessary gear and went to a nearby meadow to set up the playing field.

"So, what do you think of last night?" Byeolsu asked. "Beautiful, huh?"

"Yes, it was, Byeolsu," said Tati with a grimace. "Only the ruler of a planet could make a night that great!"

"I'm technically not the only ruler of Charybdis II nor the only in its history that has also played bainet," said Byeolsu.

Byeolsu murmured to himself and began reciting the constitutions of both Charybdis I and II. Byeolsu was a bit flustered at Tati's comment. She was just a local inhabitant of Charybdis II. He somehow managed to fall in love with her after the insurrection on Charybdis I. Everything had been going good on Charybdis II. It had been a full eight years since the insurrection on Charybdis I, and Byeolsu now can finally call Charybdis II home.

Every day to properly rule over Charybdis II, he goes to the chambers of the Imperial Council and recites the constitution of both planets. The population of Charybdis II noticed this about Byeolsu—his attentiveness to their demands and his honor. The gesture was welcomed by Byeolsu, and the evacuees turned refugees then turned citizens of Charybdis I. Charybdis II suited the Charybdisians from Charybdis I, but Charybdis II will prove a far more dangerous place then they had grown accustomed to on Charybdis I.

Byeolsu and Tati finished their game of bainet with Byeolsu winning. Tati did not say anything to Byeolsu for the rest of the day. Byeolsu did not know why.

II

The sun of Charybdis II did not beat down as harshly in the fall on the semiarid planet. Byeolsu was wandering back from a field after herding some xoynox—an animal indigenous to Charybdis II. He wondered about Tati ever since their game of bainet a couple of nights ago.

He wondered about their love. It was easy to marry an inhabitant of Charybdis II, basically a commoner back on Charybdis I. He wandered over to some caves looking over the fields he had just herder the xoynox in a while ago. Sitting down, he gathered his thoughts. After sitting down for a while, he started to pick up some pebbles and rocks and toss them around in the cave. He kept doing it until a rock hit the other side of one of the caverns, and they lit up a hologram that appeared out of thin air. Byeolsu was used to Charybdis II and did not find this hologram a threat, and he also was beginning to become well acquainted with its history. Byeolsu sat down in front of the hologram thinking it would say something or be a person. Ironically, it turned out to be an educational tool teaching a history lesson to the inhabitants of Charybdis II who used since the colony's founding.

Byeolsu listened for a bit but grew disinterested. He got up and looked to the other side. On the other side, there seemed to be old campfire remains. He shouted down the cavern.

"Anyone here?" he asked. No one responded.

He continued wondering if anyone was there. The person or group of people did not want to show their face. Byeolsu grew impatient. He knew someone was here; he just knew. He decided to go back outside. He climbed up over the cavern he was in into another one. And there he was—a Charybdisian, the people from Charybdis I. He was Byeolsu's age. Was it during the evacuation of the Charybdis I that the young man got lost? It must have been the situation. Byeolsu looked around and found a water container and quickly dashed some water on the young man's face.

The young man quickly opened his eyes and got up, startled.

"Wait? What? What just happened? I was just sleeping," he exclaimed.

"Who are you?" said Byeolsu. "You're in the middle of nowhere on Charybdis II."

"My name is Smyr," he said.

"What happened to you?" inquired Byeolsu.

"I got lost," he said, "I was on board one of the evacuation ships from Charybdis I."

Byeolsu extended his hand in friendship showing that he did not think Smyr was an enemy to deal with at the moment. Smyr contorted his face in pain as he got up from the cavern floor.

"Are you hurt?" asked Byeolsu.

"I was almost stampeded upon by some of those xoypoxes. I ran up here for safety," said Smyr.

Byeolsu thought a moment. Ever since he called Charybdis II his new home, he wondered if there were more survivors like him who were pursued by the insurrectionists. He touched his wristband to signal to personnel on Orgoz that he found a survivor.

III

◆◇◆

Byeolsu was outside the palace. Tati gave some water so the survivor. The palace was becoming cold in the late afternoon, so Tati gave the survivor a shirt.

"What's your name?" she asked. "Smyr," he said.

Byeolsu was in one of the upper rooms of the palace talking to some of the guards and captains. Eight years had passed since the insurrection on Charybdis I, and the guards and captains could not remember if other survivors had been found. Byeolsu inquired further with some of the elders from the evacuation, and they could not remember either. Byeolsu walked down to the main floor of the palace where Tati and Smyr were. For some reason, Byeolsu did not feel safe when he approached them.

"How is it going?" Byeolsu said to the two.

"He was a little cold, and I gave him some herbs for protection from a disease, but other than that, he's OK," said Tati.

Byeolsu looked at Tati. And she smiled. *Is it capricious?* he thought. Smyr was still lying on the floor. He grumbled something. Byeolsu patted Smyr on the shoulder to get up and go into one of the sleeping chambers.

"It will be dark soon. And the heat of the day escapes at night," said Byeolsu.

Smyr walked away from Byeolsu and Tati. Smyr was healthy, but he did not seem to remember how long it had been since the insurrection happened. Smyr faded into the distance.

"Do you think he remembers how long it has been since the evacuation?" asked Tati.

"Well, no need to worry, Tati. The captains and the guards said he was the only survivor found left since the evacuation," said Byeolsu.

"I wonder who he is. I mean really. Who is he? No one would survive out there alone. He seems interesting," said Tati.

Byeolsu glared at Tati. Had she gotten too cozy with Smyr? Byeolsu could not believe what he had thought. Tati touched his hand.

Byeolsu moved his hand away. Byeolsu wondered if Tati forgot who he was and his duties. Byeolsu remembered a time when he never let anyone get to close.

Smyr was in one of the upper rooms about to drift off to sleep when a misplaced wristband from one of captains started to ping. Smyr started to open his eyes. He touched the wristband.

The wristband let out an energy pulse, and it went through Smyr's body. Smyr laid still for a moment. His eyes moved rapidly around and then fixated on the ceiling. He suddenly remembers another place. A place that was not home. A place that he was taken to. He remembers fire and destruction. A voice came through the wristband and said, "I know who you are."

Smyr said, "What do you want from me? Take me back home."

"You're far away from there," said the voice. "Do you still have what I gave you?" the voice inquired further.

"How could I keep anything someone gave me?" said Smyr. "I was abandoned here. Left for dead. How did I get here?"

"That was your own doing to leave Charybdis I," said the voice. "What?" said Smyr.

The wristband sent out another pulse, and it went through Smyr's body. He remembered a place and a figure. It felt like home, but he knew it was not. He remembered getting in some kind of spacefaring ship. He was giving a bunch of things and told to keep them and that someone would be waiting for him once he reached his destination.

He did not know what happened the past eight years, but it slowly became a struggle for survival. He had kept what was told to him a secret. How did the wristband make him understand the situation more?

Smyr felt his pockets. He still had some of the items that he left with from the place he remembered. Smyr slowly laid back down on the bed and closed his eyes.

For now, Smyr slept soundly not knowing what happened and what he was told to do.

IV

Byeolsu awoke to the sounds of the guards and the captain intensely conversing. He put on his clothes and walked out to the group of captains and guards. Tati was in another room still sleeping. Byeolsu received word when he was talking to one of the captains that Smyr had left the palace. *But where to?* thought Byeolsu.

"Did he leave anything?" said Byeolsu. "No," said a captain.

"Where do you think he went to?" said Byeolsu. One of the captains shrugged his shoulders. "The plains outside the capital," he said.

Tati slowly stood beside Byeolsu, rubbing her eyes from sleep. She put on a jacket. A cool wind whipped through the palace. Tati glanced at Byeolsu; she noticed something was wrong. Byeolsu took Tati aside and told her Smyr had left the palace.

"Wait, what?" she said. "Smyr left the palace."

"Where did he go? He'll die out there," she said.

Byeolsu furrowed his brow. He started to think like Smyr. Where would he go if he was left abandoned like Smyr? Byeolsu went into the room Smyr was staying in the past night. He looked at a table and picked up a wristband. Did Smyr leave it? Byeolsu recognized the design. It was from the Imperial Council on Charybdis I. He touched it. A holographic star map popped up in the air for Byeolsu to see.

Byeolsu looked at the course of the lines drawn on the star map. They all lead from Charybdis I to Charybdis II. Byeolsu concluded the star map was not for him to see. It was made between eight and four years ago. Who was Smyr then? Byeolsu thought he was a local Charybdisian II survivor. He was left here.

He must have been left here on Charybdis II, concluded Byeolsu.

Tati walked into the room and stood beside Byeolsu. "Is everything alright?" she said.

"No," said Byeolsu. "It seems Smyr isn't from Charybdis II. He is from Charybdis I. Look!" said Byeolsu. He handed Tati the wristband.

"What is it?" she said. She touched it, and the star map popped up in front of her. She recognized the position of Charybdis II on it.

Byeolsu walked away from Tati and walked toward the captains and the guards. Tati stayed in the room. She touched the star map. Written words popped up in a holographic projection. The words were instructions. At the end of the instructions, she thought she would scream. Byeolsu was endanger.

She walked outside to hallway, but Byeolsu and the guards were not there. She gasped. What she learned she would tell no one except Byeolsu. She learned the intent behind Smyr and who he was. She did not know if Byeolsu would survive the encounter with Smyr wherever Smyr went to on Charybdis II.

V

Dirt flew in Byeolsu's face as he scaled down a ravine. He was still searching for Smyr. He was following some footprints through a ravine and a river.

Some wingless zillas flew past Byeolsu. He was catching up to Smyr. The footprints were leading to a system of caverns, which were also praying grounds for the locals.

Byeolsu wiped the sweat from his face. He made his way to the river. He wanted to take a drink of the water. When he lifted his head, he saw some smoke from the caverns below him. The river plunged into the caverns creating a waterfall. Byeolsu made his way to what looked like an abandoned encampment. He heard some murmuring in the distance. This place was holy to the locals from Charybdis II. They prayed in front of the hieroglyphics from an ancient era. Byeolsu made his way to the murmuring.

Byeolsu was only a short distance from the encampment, which was still smoldering. He spotted Smyr in the distance.

"Smyr!" he shouted. "We have been looking for you!"

"Go away," said Smyr. "You lied to me. I am not safe here."

"What do you mean? It was just you, me, and Tati yesterday," said Byeolsu. "He was right. They were right," snarled Smyr.

"Who are you talking about?" said Byeolsu.

Smyr was crouched in a praying position with his grasped hands in front of him. Before Byeolsu could move, Smyr pounced on Byeolsu. And he and Byeolsu went crashing into the smoldering encampment.

"What are you doing?" shouted Byeolsu.

Smyr's hands were on Byeolsu's face, trying to silence him. Byeolsu shoved Smyr back away from him. Smyr landed on his feet in front of Byeolsu.

"I was trying to figure out if you were a friend or not at heart," said Smyr. "Friends do not attack friends where I am from," said Byeolsu.

"Oh, really," said Smyr. "Where I come from, friends like you have already hurt me."

Byeolsu stood up and brushed off some still-smoldering embers. Luckily, he had put on some military clothes, which were resistant to the touch of fire. Byeolsu glared at Smyr.

"Whoever you are, Smyr," said Byeolsu, "the feeling isn't reciprocated to throw someone into a smoldering encampment."

"Whoever I am?" Smyr retorted.

Byeolsu furrowed his brow at Smyr. "I mean it," said Byeolsu, "I've been trying to help. Please don't ruin my gratuity."

Smyr wiped dirt off his face. "You don't think I know," said Smyr, "do you?" "No. What? And do what?" said Byeolsu in a harsh tone.

"I know what happened," said Smyr. "I know who I am supposed to be." Smyr breathed in and his chest rose with pride. This only angered Byeolsu.

"You know who you are after all this fighting and fleeing home? If that is where you are from," said Byeolsu.

"I was told I am from Charybdis I," said Smyr. "But there's more to me. That there is more than meets the eye to me. I was born on Charybdis I."

"Who told you all this?" inquired Byeolsu. "Enceladus told me," said Smyr.

"How do you know that name?" Byeolsu immediately became tense all over his body. What had Enceladus done to Smyr? Had he murdered Smyr's family like his?

"What did Enceladus do to you? What did he tell you?" said Byeolsu.

Smyr grimaced. "He told me I am the future ruler of Charybdis I," said Smyr. "What? He's lying," said Byeolsu.

"He told you that to get your attention and trick you to do something," said Byeolsu.

Byeolsu looked over at the hieroglyphics on the cavern walls. Shadows leapt back and forth between the ancient writings. A zilla cawed in the cavern. Byeolsu did not have time to hear Smyr's story. However, Smyr came to know Enceladus's name. It must be taken seriously by the guards and captains of Charybdis II.

"We need to get back to the palace," said Byeolsu. "Are you done fighting me?" "Yes, I am," said Byeolsu. He grinned.

Byeolsu touched his wristband. Smyr glanced at the wristband. "I have one just like that," said Smyr.

"You never stop with your storytelling, do you?" said Byeolsu. "No, it's not a story. It's a fact," said Smyr.

"Alright," said Byeolsu, "We need to make it back to the palace before nightfall.

I am touching the wristband to call some guards here."

Smyr agreed to ride back to the palace. The guards showed up a little bit before nightfall. Byeolsu and Smyr kept their fight a secret. They disembarked from the hovercraft. The guards were walking around the palace. Byeolsu and Smyr quickly went to their respective rooms in the palace.

VI

In the morning, the palace was buzzing with locals wanting food for their first meal of the day. The guards started to brush them aside. Byeolsu was still sleeping until he heard the call of a zilla, which was perched on a tree outside his palace window. As Byeolsu woke up, he rubbed his eyes and heard the commotion outside his palace room. He wondered about Tati. He must tell her about Smyr knowing the name of Enceladus and claiming he was from Charybdis I. He went outside to the hallway.

"What is all the noise about in the palace?" Byeolsu inquired to a guard.

"Some of the locals received premonitions about famine and war coming," said one of the guards. "They are frightened."

Byeolsu knew some of the local superstitious were not superstitious at all. The locals claim to have the power for premonitions, and prophecies were well attested to by the records, which were formerly on Charybdis I inside the Imperial Council. Byeolsu thought Tati was one of them: a seer. He walked into the front of the palace. He sat down for the first meal of the day.

Tati was in the room where the first meal of the day was being served. She ignored Byeolsu. She was writing using Byeolsu's wristband in the air. Technology was sparse on Charybdis II, but the locals of Charybdis II kept knowledge and have memories of having technology. *They are simply not nomads after all*, Byeolsu thought.

"Hello," said Byeolsu.

Tati looked away perturbed. Byeolsu put his hand on her knee.

"So, are you ready for the day? How was your night's sleep?" asked Byeolsu. "I had a dream," said Tati.

"Of what?" asked Byeolsu.

"First, what did Smyr tell you when you went looking for him?" asked Tati. "He's yet to wake up," said Byeolsu. Smyr walked into the room. "On second thought, there he is," said Byeolsu, knowing Smyr could not hear him. "We need to go to Charybdis I," said Tati.

"What? You never have been to my home world," said Byeolsu.

"I know," said Tati. She gazed at Byeolsu. She did not tell him about looking at Smyr's wristband. She looked over at Smyr. He was wearing the wristband. She gazed again at Byeolsu.

"We need to take Smyr too," said Tati. "Why?" Byeolsu glared.

"It's not fair. It's not fair what they did to him," said Tati. "Whatever they did to him is beside the point. He's one of us, a local and refugee."

Byeolsu sensed Tati was not telling him everything. And she wasn't. Tati looked away and her lip slightly quivered. She did not tell him the secrets she learned on Smyr's wristband.

Byeolsu liked Tati. He liked her a lot despite her being from a nameless group of nomads. What was he going to do? Byeolsu winced at the decision he just made.

"Well," said Byeolsu, "we'll go. We'll take some guards with us and have a captain take us there. The sleeping chambers have been maintained, so no worry about the length of the trip."

Byeolsu took his hand way from Tati and let out a sigh. He really did not want to go to Charybdis I. *The answer to Smyr*, he thought, *is on Charybdis II*. Despite being on Charybdis II for the past eight years, he called it home. The insurrectionists as far as he knew were still on Charybdis I, but their forces have been scattering as resistance from the refugees increased. Where Enceladus was, he did not know. Even though he murdered one of his friends, one of his protectors, back on Charybdis I, it was above Byeolsu to hold a bitterness to Enceladus. For all he knew, he was dead. The army probably killed him as they advanced on the capital.

VII

The morning Tati, Smyr, and Byeolsu were to board one of the spacefaring ships to Charybdis I, it was breezy. Tati was robed in traditional attire, but one of her fists was clenched. Smyr looked like he was more in his head than anything contemplating his future. Byeolsu was walking and talking to a group of guards. Tati parted ways with them. She went to the opposite side of the ship where a sleeping chamber was ready for her. She waited patiently for one of the guards.

Smyr was one of the first to ready himself for the sleeping chamber, but before he got in the chamber, Tati walked up to him.

"I'm glad you agreed to going to Charybdis I," she said.

Smyr did not respond. Tati thought about his wristband and all the secrets she read and the intent behind Smyr. *When will it be revealed?* she thought. She watched him lay himself into the chamber. Before one of the guards began to program the chamber for sleep, Tati slipped her hand into the sleeping chamber and put a device behind Smyr's ear to both track him and find out more secrets. The device would track him physically once they reach Charybdis I, and it would download his thoughts during his sleep.

She went against Byeolsu's wishes to take action with Smyr. She was doing it for her type though. With the knowledge of Smyr's wristband, she wanted to know more why he was on Charybdis II. She did not feel safe with Byeolsu and was becoming too close to him. Once they reached Charybdis I, he will start to remember past acquaintances and how happy he was. She wiped a tear form her eye. A guard touched her shoulder to escort her to a sleeping chamber. She turned and followed. Byeolsu entered his sleeping chamber too. Shortly thereafter, the ship lifted off the ground and disappeared into the purple and orange air of a sunset on Charybdis II.

They woke up on Charybdis I just as planned. Tati was the first to touch Charybdis I's soil, and she did without Byeolsu. She breathed in the air. It was similar to Charybdis II's air. Smyr was right behind her. She moved away from Smyr so her back was not to him.

Byeolsu emerged from the ship. He scratched his head. He knew where to take Tati. He would take her to the beach where some hieroglyphics can be found. He would leave Smyr to wander. Byeolsu was not convinced Tati was a seer and wanted to know more about what Smyr was up too.

He called one of the guards over to get a hovercraft. A little while later, a hovercraft appeared, and all three boarded to take them to their destinations. Byeolsu left Smyr at the capital of Orleans. It was just Byeolsu and Tati now. Byeolsu looked at Tati with eager eyes. Tati averted her gaze. The hovercraft landed at the beach. The two disembarked.

"Follow me," said Byeolsu. And Tati did. "Where are you taking me?" said Tati.

"I'm taking you to place I often visited when I was a child," said Byeolsu.

Tati did not respond. It was the afternoon on Charybdis I, and Tati was taken aback by how crisp and humid the air was after coming from the capital. Byeolsu and Tati made their way through some overgrowth to the bottom of cliff. Tati looked up at the cliff as Byeolsu continued to make his way a little farther to the other side.

She began an attempt to read some of the hieroglyphics on her own. "Can you understand any of these?" she said to Byeolsu.

"Of course. There are prophecies here about the inhabitants of Charybdis I. The hieroglyphics even contain prophecies about my family," said Byeolsu. Tati began to murmur some of the hieroglyphics. She could understand them. Tati stopped murmuring. She did not want Byeolsu to know she could understand the hieroglyphics. Byeolsu was too excited explaining the hieroglyphics to Tati. Could Byeolsu not hear and see and understand what she meant? She could sense the sparks of the interest in one another fade away in the difference of understanding the hieroglyphics.

VIII

Tati was suspicious of Byeolsu now and even more suspicious of Byeolsu's home world. They were still at the hieroglyphics by the beach. Tati took her hand off one of the hieroglyphics. "So, what do you think?" said Byeolsu.

Tati knew she must say something to not give away she is no longer interested in Byeolsu. She was angered at what she was reading, and now that she was getting to know Byeolsu more by the moment, the more fears grew and the more humiliated she became that Charybdis I and Charybdis II were somehow inextricably linked. She still pitied Byeolsu. How did he get over all this fighting and the loss of his family? Byeolsu motioned to Tati to move away from the cliff. As they both moved away from the cliff, they glanced at one another.

Tati was after Smyr now. Her intuition about him was confirmed here on Charybdis I, she thought. Whatever happened to Smyr was not his fault nor was it fair. Tati and Smyr reached the bottom of the cliff.

"Let's go and look for Smyr," Tati said to Byeolsu. "Alright, let's go find him," said Byeolsu.

Tati and Byeolsu walked to the hovercraft but did not find Smyr. Byeolsu asked one of the guards where he could be, but the guard did not know. Byeolsu and Tati grew frustrated. He had not used his wristband and the power of the Charybdis I's technology yet, but he finally relented. He touched his wristband, and holographic projection showed up of Charybdis I. Smyr was somewhere near the capital. *What is he doing there?* thought Byeolsu.

Tati turned her back to Byeolsu while he was looking at the projection. Tati touched her wrist, and her own wristband became visible again. She too found the location of Smyr. Tati kept thinking about her family and her kind back on Charybdis II. *How can Charybdis I and Charybdis II be linked?* she thought. She knew not even Byeolsu knew both of the worlds' histories that well.

The capital was far from the hovercraft landed. Tati and Byeolsu would have to hike to the capital. Byeolsu was surprised Smyr went by foot to the capital.

"You could have ordered one of the guards to take the hovercraft to the capital," she said.

Byeolsu heard Tati, but he was more concerned about what he knew about Smyr from back on Charybdis II. He knew without the help of the guards he would have to scope out where Smyr had gone to see if he left more clues. Hopefully, they would reach Smyr by nightfall. Byeolsu wanted to put up camp just outside the capital.

As they made their way through the woods, they could hear the calls of the wilderness surrounding them. Byeolsu thought about Tati. He put his arm around her to comfort her. Tati pushed him away every time. Byeolsu became defensive and dissatisfied all at once. Who did she think she was? He was only letting her close to him as they both got dragged into the situation further with Smyr.

IX

Upon reaching the capital, Tati and Byeolsu looked for some water. No one near them was inside past the walls of the capital. Leaves whirled around both of them as they made their way through the city.

The chambers of the Imperial Council lay before them as they were currently on the uppermost part of a hill by the entrance to the capital. They both gazed at what was before them. The city was still as it had been abandoned. An insurrectionist ship floated in the distance above the city. For now, no one knew they were here.

"Let's head to the Imperial Library," said Byeolsu. "I'll bet we will find who Smyr actually is there." Byeolsu smiled at Tati. Behind the smile was his knowledge that Smyr knew who Enceladus was. The insurrectionist who murdered his friend Sirius. Byeolsu started to ignore Tati, the memory of Sirius jarring his emotions.

They both walked into the library. The archives were as long and deep as the eye could see. Byeolsu's race had chronicled everything through their long journey through time. Tati looked amazed.

"How many archives are there?" she said to Byeolsu. "From every world my people encountered," said Byeolsu.

They were in an aisle of the archives when they heard a noise. Both Tati and Byeolsu stood still. After a while, Byeolsu motioned to Tati to go outside of the library. It was there that they saw Smyr for the first time. He was throwing rocks against the wall of the library.

Tati was still robed, so she was hiding her wristband from both Smyr and Byeolsu. Byeolsu clinched both of his fists. Smyr's back was to both Byeolsu and Tati. Smyr dropped a group of rocks and slowly turned to Byeolsu and Tati.

"You know," he said, "you could have brought one of the guards to make it known you were arriving." He smirked.

"You seem satisfied," Byeolsu said. "I am," said Smyr.

"Now, how did you know the name of Enceladus?" said Byeolsu. He quickly looked at Tati. She seemed to absorb what Byeolsu just said. Tati still had her hands beneath her robe. Byeolsu grabbed a knife from the side of his leg.

He held it in the air at level with Smyr's face. Smyr did not blink. He tossed a wristband in the air.

"You still don't believe I am from here," said Smyr. "I can't believe you said that," said Byeolsu.

Tati looked at both of them. It was obvious a fight was starting between them. But where did she stand? She touched the wristband and neural link was established and began downloading Smyr's thoughts. With the neural link, she could outdo Smyr in a fight knowing Smyr's actions before striking her. Tati took a step back from the two.

Byeolsu lunged at Smyr. Smyr instantly moved to the side and grabbed Byeolsu's arm, making him drop the knife. Smyr whipped Byeolsu around to put his arm behind his back. Tati brought her hands beneath the robe into the light and in her hands were weapons from her home world. Seeing the threat, Smyr released Byeolsu and went after Tati, but Tati blocked Smyr instantaneously pushing Smyr to the ground. While Smyr was on the ground, she touched her wristband and began downloading more of Smyr's thoughts. She found out that recently he was with someone, but who?

X

━━◆◇◆━━

Tati stood in fear. She was almost paralyzed with fear from what she learned about Smyr. She felt the instinct to run and she did. Tati began to wipe tears from eyes as she ran. She ran what seemed like forever until she reached the entrance of the capital. Tati could not help but thin.k of her kind back at home. As a woman, thoughts of pity began streaming through her mind about the shadowy person and people behind Smyr. She still believed that Smyr was innocent. How Byeolsu would handle Smyr, Tati did not know. A feeling of betrayal shook Tati as she began making her way through the woods to the hovercraft.

Smyr was still holding Byeolsu's arm. Byeolsu put one of his legs behind Smyr's legs. He threw Smyr off balance, releasing the grip Smyr had of him. Byeolsu jumped a few feet away from Smyr. He composed himself and took a look around him. Tati was gone. Byeolsu felt betrayed.

"Now that your woman has left you," said Smyr, "what are you going to do?

Kill me just for knowing someone's name?"

"I want to know why you are here, and for you to go back where you came from," said Byeolsu.

"To go back where I came from," said Smyr. "Well that was the right statement after all!"

The buildings surrounding Smyr and Byeolsu were casting shadows on them as the two binary stars of Charybdis I fell below the horizon. It was about to be nightfall. Smyr glared at Byeolsu. Byeolsu was ready for what Smyr had to say to him.

As nightfall began to approach and one of the moons cast light on the capital, Byeolsu eyes fixated on Smyr; and as soon as he did, the shadows came to life. Byeolsu's eyes widened with fear for a bit, but then he grew more confident.

Someone was coming at him. A hand emerged from shadows. Byeolsu watched closely. The shadows coalesced into none other than Enceladus.

As soon as Byeolsu recognized Enceladus, he threw the knife at him. But to Byeolsu's dismay, the knife went through and the image of Enceladus shimmered before him. It was a more advanced holographic image than Byeolsu had ever encountered. Byeolsu looked around. Three to four insurrectionist ships had flanked the capital.

"I take it you have spotted me, Smyr and Enceladus," said Byeolsu. "Now tell me who you are even though it seems you are about to kill me."

"Why don't you tell him yourself, Smyr, who you are," said Enceladus.

Smyr's lips quivered. It looked like he did not know now what to say to Byeolsu.

"Isn't this always what you wanted to say, Smyr, since we met?" said Enceladus. Byeolsu was puzzled at the interchange between the two.

"All I know of you, Smyr, is that you somehow knew the name of Enceladus," said Byeolsu. "Remember, you were found on Charybdis II."

Smyr remained quiet. He only knew the facts he learned at the library. Smyr started to shame himself for what he was about to say.

"I'm your replacement," said Smyr to Byeolsu. "You're my what?" asked Byeolsu

"Yes," said Smyr, "I was born on Charybdis I, but my family was tricked into being a group of spies before you and I were born Byeolsu," said Smyr.

Byeolsu winced. He had only heard of people spying from stories and what he learned in the capital's library growing up with his family. Enceladus did not seem to swell with pride but only hid further beneath the holographic projection.

"So not just you, but your family was also manipulated to attack Charybdis I. Why?" said Byeolsu.

"I don't know the answer," said Smyr. He felt an invisible pain at knowing that his family may not be his family after all. Enceladus was the final link to who Smyr is.

"Then who is, Smyr?" said Byeolsu to Enceladus.

"He wasn't just your replacement Byeolsu. Nor is his family. He is from what they call genetic material to replace the rulers of Charybdis I. It's from a place you have only heard of Byeolsu. It is called Earth," said Enceladus.

"We were tired of this oppression, Byeolsu," said Enceladus. "Grant it, you were never at fault, Byeolsu.

You were two young to hold responsibility. I am now giving you the chance to join our side."

"What? I would never. There are still innocent people on Charybdis I and II," said Byeolsu.

Smyr stepped out of the holographic projection of Enceladus's hand. He was unsure of where this was going as Enceladus said more to Byeolsu. Smyr still wanted to know what happened to his family.

Smyr turned around to face Enceladus. "I want to know what happed to my family. I want to know why I ended up on Charybdis II alone and left to die," said Smyr.

Enceladus's features on his face did not budge. "You killed them, didn't you?" said Smyr. "They died for a worthy cause," said Enceladus

"You just could not get enough that you killed my family. And now you killed some kind of bastard meant to replace me and the rulers of Charybdis I," said Byeolsu in anger. The holographic image of Enceladus faded. Byeolsu and Smyr heard footsteps. Byeolsu and Smyr put their backs to one another. From the moonlight, they saw soldiers from the ships. Enceladus sent them to kill Smyr and Byeolsu. Who would when this fight, they both did not know.

XI

"Do you think we'll make it out of here, Smyr?" asked to Byeolsu.

They both were quickly surrounded by Enceladus's soldiers. Both Smyr and Byeolsu took a fighting stance. "This fight is going to be over quick," said Byeolsu.

Byeolsu touched his wristband, and it automatically emitted a shock wave around Smyr and Byeolsu. The soldiers were down automatically. They looked around. As soon as they realized they both were safe, Smyr and Byeolsu sprinted away from one another. Byeolsu wondered what he was going to do with Smyr now. *Enceladus did not just leave me to die this time*, thought Byeolsu, *he wanted to kill me.*

"Whatever Enceladus unleashed must be a threat to him," said Byeolsu. "Why me?" said Smyr.

"We must leave the capital and find Tati," said Smyr.

Byeolsu could only but wonder what was going through Tati's head. Was she still on Byeolsu's side? Smyr started to walk behind Byeolsu.

Smyr pondered what Enceladus said to both Byeolsu and him. He said Smyr was from Charybdis I, but not from it at the same time. *What did he mean by the place called Earth?* Smyr wondered.

By the time Smyr finished pondering what was said to him in the heart of the city, they had reached the entrance of the capital. Byeolsu massaged his shoulder with his hand as he just noticed it was strained during the fighting. Smyr too patted himself down and brushed off debris from the fighting. Byeolsu and Smyr looked up to the night sky above them. Some of the insurrectionist ships were disappearing into the clouds.

"Are they going to space?" said Smyr.

"I don't know," said Byeolsu. "It seems they have taken all they can take from Charybdis I."

"Where is Tati?" asked Smyr.

"We need to make our way through the forest back to the hovercraft and then to the ship," said Byeolsu.

Smyr and Byeolsu left the capital and made their way through the forest. Byeolsu looked for any signs of Tati in the forest or signs that she had been taken by Enceladus. Once they made their way through the forest, they came to where the hovercraft was. Byeolsu and Smyr could both see downed guards from the ship besides the hovercraft. A fight had taken place. Byeolsu and Smyr stood at the back of the hovercraft where the ship's doorway was opened.

Tati was seen in the front of the ship touching some of the controls. Byeolsu stepped into the hovercraft. He made some noise, making it known to Tati that he was there in the hovercraft.

"Tati, what you have done I have forgiven you," said Byeolsu. "They're after my people," Tati cried.

"That may be true, but step away from the controls," said Byeolsu.

Tati continued to sob as she stepped away from the controls. She walked to Byeolsu. And she fell into his arms. Smyr noticed the guards were waking up and moved into the hovercraft.

"Byeolsu, the guards are waking," said Smyr. "They need to take your orders." "I know where those ships above the capital are going," said Tati. "They're going to Charybdis II."

"How do you know this?" said Byeolsu.

"I spied on Smyr," said Tati. "I tagged him with a mind-reading device. I know his secret. He is not fully one of us. He's from another world."

"Yes, I know," said Byeolsu.

Smyr now was beside Tati and Smyr. He more than knew they were talking about him. He looked around the hovercraft. The guards were already at the back waiting for orders.

Byeolsu let go of Tati and went to the guards. He composed himself and tried to look like the ruler he always should have been and still is in the eyes of Charybdisians. He looked at all the guards that stood before him.

"We need to get the hovercraft back to the ship," said Byeolsu to the guards. "And we need to make our way to Charybdis II.'

"But, Byeolsu, we were attacked by Tati. She must face consequences to her actions," said the guard.

"She may," said Byeolsu. "But first, we need to make it back to Charybdis II."

Byeolsu went back over to Tati and took her to sit back down in the back of the hovercraft. The guards went to the front of the ship where the controls were. Smyr sat in the back of the hovercraft with Byeolsu and

Tati. The hovercraft slowly rose from Charybdis I. In short time, they were back onboard a ship headed to Charybdis II. Byeolsu had found the secret to Smyr. Tati too found the secret, but what she found affected her far more deeply.

XII

The ship Smyr, Tati, and Byeolsu were in arrived at Charybdis II. They were a short distance from the palace and were at one of the docks attended by the military of Charybdis I. All three awoke from hyper sleep. Byeolsu walked toward the guards who were holding a communication device. Word was getting out about Tati's actions, and everything that happened on Charybdis II.

"Tati needs to come before chiefs in the government on Charybdis II and the military of Charybdis I," said the guard.

Smyr was seen walking toward the palace in the far distance. Tati sat on the footsteps of the dock and never looked at anyone but just stared at the horizon. The guards and a few captains milled about Byeolsu.

Byeolsu considered contacting the palace about what has happened and alerting a nearby chief of Charybdis II, but before he did, the ships at the dock began to shake. Some guards began shouting at Byeolsu and others. They were surprised by the shaking and someone shouted insurrectionist ships had been spotted and now were attacking the palace. They seemed not to notice the docks.

Tati stood and started to run across the plains to some of her kind to see what was going on with the sudden arrival of the ships. She could not believe what her kind were saying. Messages were being relayed throughout Charybdis II that insurrectionist ships came to exterminate who lived on Charybdis II.

Byeolsu did not care about Tati. She was better off with her people. As for Smyr, he now knew the plot of Smyr, Enceladus, and the insurrectionist. The plot had been to overthrow Byeolsu no matter what and gain the power of Charybdisians with the known universe and further powers.

Byeolsu summoned his military to take him to the palace and surrounding areas. Charybdis II must not fall to Enceladus and the insurrectionists. Byeolsu alerted even more military ships throughout Charybdis II, in orbit, and in the area of the plains.

When Byeolsu and his military moved upon the palace, he could not believe what he was seeing or what he was about to do. Byeolsu quickly ordered his guards to the library inside the palaces and into any of the sacred places. Byeolsu saw some seeing nomads inside the palace and in the sacred places.

"We need to go," said Byeolsu to some of the seeing nomads. Byeolsu let the seeing nomads run to safety. Byeolsu ran to one of the guards. The guards were communicating to the rest of the ships and the military.

Byeolsu saw tears of frustration run down one of the guard's faces. He looked over at Byeolsu and handed him some communique. Byeolsu looked through them— Charybdis II was beginning to fall to the insurrectionist.

"We must get you to safety, Byeolsu," said one of the captains.

"Where?" said Byeolsu. "Enceladus and the insurrectionists are after what remains of the Charybdisians."

"The Charybdisian known universe is at stake," said one of the captains to Byeolsu.

"But the prophecies about Byeolsu and the rulers of the Charybdisians," said one of the guards.

"We have no time to bring this up, and I know what he is after," said Byeolsu. "What is he after, Byeolsu?" said the captain who was about to give orders to the military and the ships.

"He's after what Charybdisians have ruled over for millennia in our known universe," said Byeolsu.

"But that is only two planets," said an officer. "Then, they're after something more. They're after our knowledge presently and what came before us."

"Yes, I know," said Byeolsu. "They're after a place that has only been mentioned in our prophecies and lore. It's a place called Earth."

XIII

Byeolsu was on board one of the ships, which was a part of the fleet. Some of the locals from Charybdis II were also on board. Byeolsu started to look for Tati, but she was not found. Byeolsu was taken to the front of the ship to command what remained of the military.

"We must follow them to Earth," said Byeolsu.

The people of Charybdis had never used the power of their universe in millennia to reach Earth, Byeolsu thought. It was part of lore and prophecies. Earth happened so long ago. Enceladus's and the insurrectionists sudden appearance was now somehow connected to their destination of Earth.

Byeolsu crouched in front of a seer. Some of the locals huddled around several seers hoping to quell their fright. Byeolsu touched the shoulders of the seer.

"What can you perceive?" asked Byeolsu.

"The end of the insurrectionists has come. That's why they have wanted to control lives of Charybdisians," said the seer.

"Why are they going to Earth?" asked Byeolsu. "It's been so long ago that our peoples met Earth."

"Indeed, it is at the edge of our known universe," said the seer. "It's only reachable at the edge of our universe. The edge of time and space itself."

Byeolsu left the seer. Indeed, the edge of space and time itself was nothing new to the people who studied the prophecies and lore of Charybdis I and II. Byeolsu stood by one of the captains.

A group of insurrectionist ships were ahead of them, but soon they began to blur into beams of light. Byeolsu felt the change in space and time around him. No matter what was about to happen, he knew he must reach Earth.